Written and Illustrated
by SANAE ISHIDA

Ba-chan
the Ninja Grandma

An Adventure with
Little Kunoichi the Ninja Girl

little bigfoot
an imprint of sasquatch books
seattle, wa

On a super secret island in a super, super secret village . . . .

there is a one-of-a-kind ninja treehouse.

BUNNY'S GARDEN

LITTLE KUNOICHI'S ROOM

BUNNY'S SUITE

NIN-JUTSU TRAINING ROOM

KITCHEN/DINING

BABY BRO'S ROOM

PARENTS' ROOMS

LIVING ROOM

INSIDE THE NINJA TREEHOUSE

This is the home of Little Kunoichi, her family, and her pet, Bunny.
Summer vacation is nearly over.

Little Kunoichi and Bunny have explored every nook
and cranny of the island.

BEEN THERE

They've played with every toy and game a squillion times.

DONE THAT

They are bored, bored . . .

BORED!!!

Little Kunoichi has some ideas to spice things up.

Mom and Dad have a better idea.

Quirky and wise, Little Kunoichi's grandma—known as Ba-chan—lives on a nearby island that she built HERSELF. She calls it Kame (*kah-meh*) Shima, which means "Turtle Isle." She likes turtles.

RECYCLING GENIUS

Anything is possible with Ba-chan!
The kids are excited for the visit!

Where are Little Kunoichi, Baby Bro, and Bunny?
They are shopping at the market to buy Ba-chan an
omiyage (oh-mi-yah-geh), which is a special kind of gift.

A ninja must never visit another ninja's home without a present.

SUPER SECRET
ISLAND

It's a hop, skip, and a *mizugumo* jump from the super secret island to Kame Shima!

Look, there's Ba-chan!

WOW, THESE MIZUGUMO
SHOES REALLY FLOAT!

KAME SHIM

Ba-chan is delighted
to see them.

SUNGLASSES!
I LOVE THEM.
ARIGATO!

THEY COME WITH
ACCESSORIES.

First, Ba-chan feeds them a hearty home-cooked meal. Noodles and rice balls and seaweed, oh my! Soba and *dango* and *shabu-shabu* too! And Ba-chan always remembers their favorite treat: animal-shaped mochi tempura.

CATCH!

Then she takes them to her workshop.
It's messy and wild and full of
wondrous creations.

With Ba-chan, ideas and experiments flow endlessly.

Baby Bro swallows a remote that activates a transformation function.

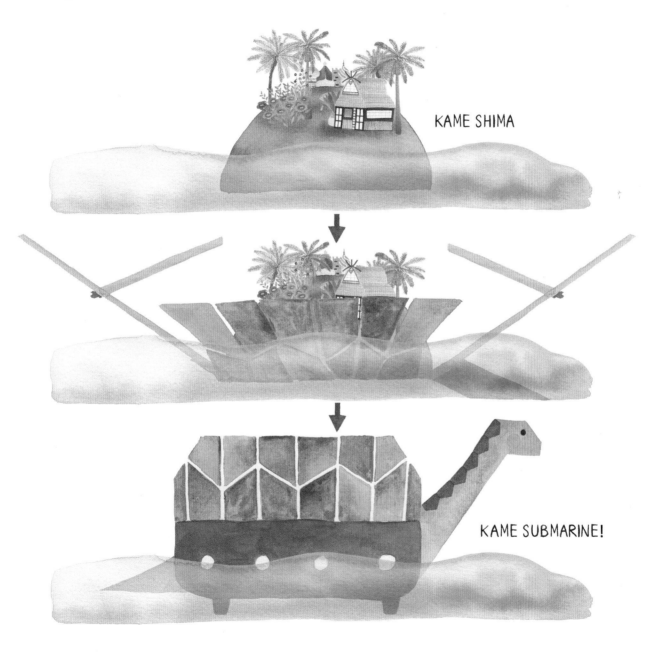

KAME SHIMA

KAME SUBMARINE!

Holy ninja! The island turns into a submarine!

Deep, deep down goes the Kame Submarine.
Seven minutes and seventy leagues later, they
see a giant dome. It's one of Ba-chan's latest
projects—an underwater amusement park!

So many rides and attractions! They start with the Mirror Maze of Yen. It's tricky to complete the maze without getting distracted by the magical mirrors that reveal desires!

They spend the day exploring . . .

and exploring.

SUDDENLY Baby Bro's tummy rumbles.

UH-OH, DO YOU HAVE TO...??

RUMBLE
RUMBLE

"Quick!" says Ba-chan. "The transformation function might get activated again, back to the Kame Sub!"

They make it back above water, safe and sound.

Little Kunoichi is curious.

BA-CHAN, WHY DID YOU BUILD THE TREASURE TROVE?

WELL, I NOTICED THAT GROWN-UPS TREAT MONEY LIKE IT'S MORE VALUABLE THAN ANYTHING ELSE, AND I HAD SO MANY QUESTIONS!

IS IT TRUE? WHY? WHAT'S REALLY VALUABLE?

MONEY IS LIKE AN AMUSEMENT PARK—FULL OF UPS AND DOWNS AND MYSTERIOUS WHIRL-AROUNDS.

I CREATED THE TREASURE TROVE TO GET MORE KNOWLEDGE AND SUPER MOOLA NINJA SKILLS!

ALSO! I MADE A SHIGIN POEM. YOU KNOW, ONE OF THOSE SING-SONGY, OLD-TIMEY POEMS. HERE, HAVE A LISTEN.

AHEM HEM

MI MI MI

MONEY, MOOLA, MAZUMA
A SIMPLE TOOL TO USE
"MORE IS BETTER"
"NOT ENOUGH"
BEWARE THE WORDS YOU CHOOSE

CURRENCY IS VALUABLE
AND GOLD CAN BUY A LOT
SO EXCITING!
SHINY TOO!
BUT ALL CANNOT BE BOUGHT

WHAT TRULY FLOWS AND GROWS AND GROWS
WON'T FILL THE MARKET STALLS
WHAT MATTERS MOST
IN THE END
IS NOT FOR SALE AT ALL

WE'RE SO ABUNDANT, FULL OF LIGHT
AGLOW LIKE FIREFLIES
WE ALL POSSESS
GEMS GALORE
PERCEIVED WITH MORE THAN EYES...

WHAT ARE YOUR HIDDEN GEMS?
THAT'S FOR YOU TO DISCOVER AND
IT'S A VERY SPECIAL TREASURE HUNT!

C'MON, I'VE GOT
SOME IDEAS TO
GET YOU STARTED!

For the rest of the visit, they all practice many forms of valuable *nin-jutsu* (*nin* = ninja, *jutsu* = skills).

GARDENING-JUTSU

CULINARY-JUTSU

YUM! NUNCHUCK AND STAR COOKIES!

CONSTRUCTION-JUTSU
(WITH RECYCLED MATERIALS)

BRAVO!!

NINJA APPLIANCES

Refrig

NAPPING-JUTSU

GROUP-HUG-JUTSU

TRAMPOLINE-JUTSU

NICE FLIP!

Too soon, it's their last night with Ba-chan. Together they build a fire, roast *taiyaki*, and dance under the stars.

Every one of us
Has priceless inner magic
Made of things like these:

Curiosity,
Resourcefulness, kindness, love,
Imagination!

Yen is the official currency of Japan. The word is based on *en*, which means "round." (Get it? Coins are round.) In English, the word *yen* means a craving or desire.

Mochi is a rice cake made from short-grain sticky rice that is pounded into a paste.

Giving gifts, especially food, is a large part of Japanese culture. An *omiyage* is often a souvenir from travels.

Taiyaki is a fish-shaped cake usually filled with sweet red-bean paste.

In Japan, *chan* is added to a name as a term of endearment, as in *Ba-chan*.

Bonsai is an ancient Japanese art form of growing trees in containers, dating back at least one thousand years.

Did you know?

Koban is an oval-shape gold coin that was used as currency during the Edo period in Japan between 1603 and 1868.

Soba are buckwheat noodles usually served in a soup.

Shabu-shabu is a hot pot dish that got its name because the thinly sliced meat and vegetables cooking in a boiling broth sounded like "shabu shabu."

Portuguese people living in Nagasaki introduced the Japanese to *tempura*, or fritters, and popularized this deep-fried battered vegetable and seafood dish.

Mizugumo translates to "water spider" and was a floating device that ninjas strapped to their feet to cross bodies of water.

Dango is a sweet dumpling made out of rice flour.

For the
original
Ba-chan

Manufactured in China by C&C Offset Printing Co. Ltd. Shenzhen,
Guangdong Province, in May 2018

Published by Little Bigfoot, an imprint of Sasquatch Books

22 21 20 19 18   9 8 7 6 5 4 3 2 1

Editor: Christy Cox
Production editor: Em Gale
Design: Bryce de Flamand

Library of Congress Cataloging-in-Publication Data
Names: Ishida, Sanae, author, illustrator.
  Title: Ba-chan the ninja grandma : an adventure with Little Kunoichi, the
    ninja girl / Sanae Ishida.
  Description: Seattle : Little Bigfoot, [2018] | Summary: Little Kunoichi, a
    young ninja, finds adventure when she spends the day with her inventor
    grandmother.
  Identifiers: LCCN 2018000269 | ISBN 9781632171184 (hardcover)
  Subjects: | CYAC: Ninja--Fiction. | Grandmothers--Fiction.
  Classification: LCC PZ7.1.I84 Bac 2018 | DDC [E]--dc23
  LC record available at https://lccn.loc.gov/2018000269

ISBN: 978-1-63217-118-4

Sasquatch Books
1904 Third Avenue, Suite 710
Seattle, WA 98101
(206) 467-4300
SasquatchBooks.com